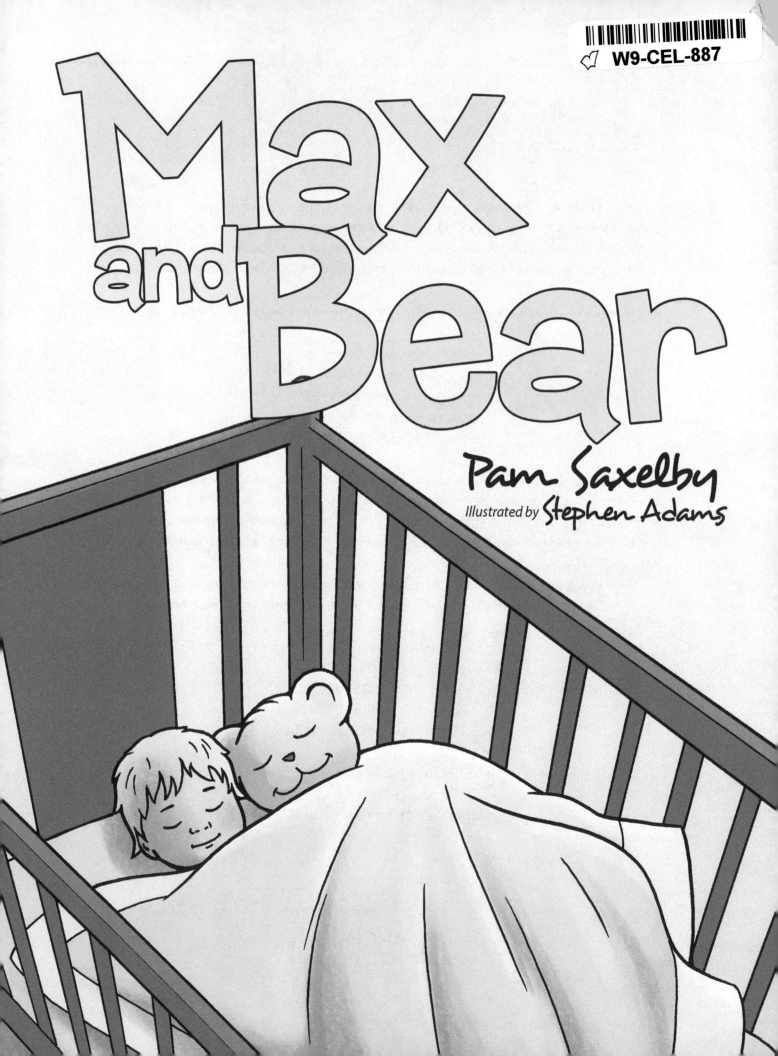

Max and Bear

Pam Saxelby

Illustrated by Stephen Adams

Archway Publishing books may be ordered through booksellers or by contacting:

Archway Publishing
1663 Liberty Drive
Bloomington, IN 47403
www.archwaypublishing.com
1-(888)-242-5904

ISBN: 978-1-4808-0790-7 (sc)
ISBN: 978-1-4808-0792-1 (hc)
ISBN: 978-1-4808-0791-4 (e)

Printed in the United States of America

Archway Publishing rev. date: 06/05/2014

"For Max"

With special thanks to my
entire family and to EG

Bear had been
waiting for Max.

Bear was given to Patrick, Max's Dad by Big Sam at a party. Max wasn't there yet. He was still busy growing in his Mommy's tummy.

Max arrived on November 30th. Everyone was glad the waiting was over especially Bear!

At Bear's new home, Max's crib, he met Sophie the giraffe, an overstuffed Scottie dog, and a turtle. Oh, Bear also met a goofy looking monkey, but he didn't last long. The real Scotties took care of him!

Bear was patient, but when Max's Mommy picked up Sophie the giraffe, he was disappointed.

Sophie was brown and white and she squeaked. Bear was plain blue, and soft. He did not squeak.

Max liked Sophie. He could bite her leg, her head or even her tummy and Sophie squeaked happily. Sophie went with Max everywhere. They went to the park, on long walks, to restaurants, and even on the subway.

Bear waited.

Max got **bigger**.

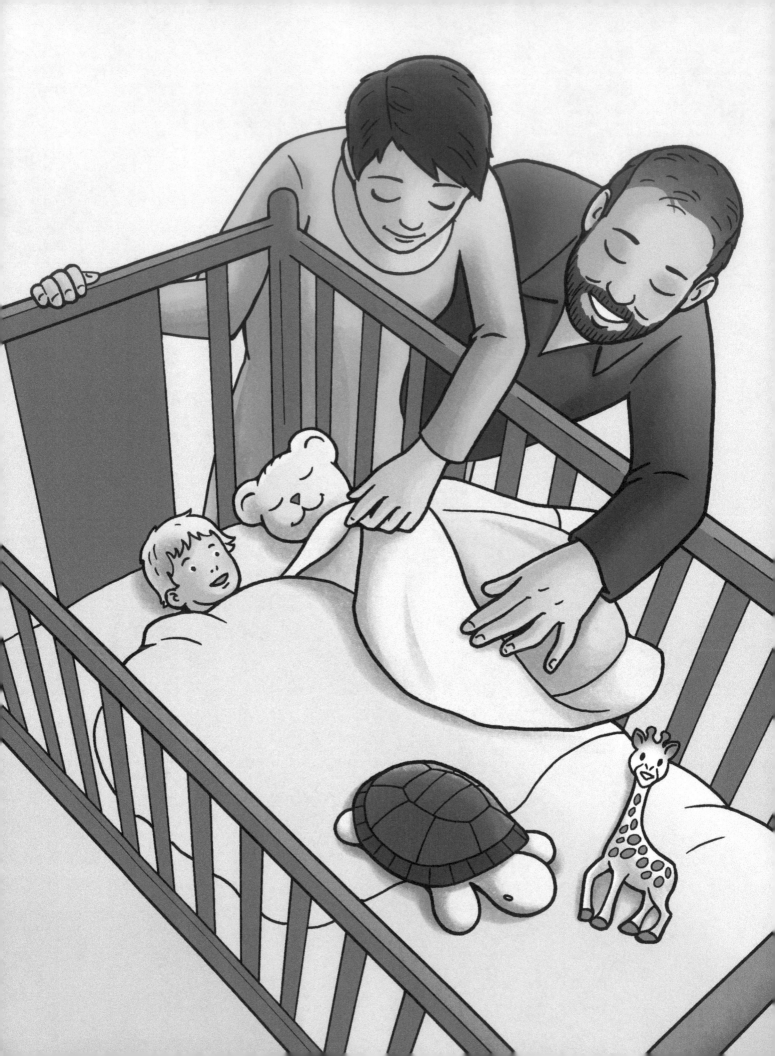

Max's Mom and Dad decided Max was big enough to move out of his bassinet and sleep in his crib. Bear was excited!

"Now," Bear thought, Max will see me!" But, Max did not notice Bear.

Max spied Turtle. When Max's Mom pushed a button on Turtle, magical things happened. Turtle played music, and his shell lit Max's room with hundreds of twinkling lights that sparkled like stars. Max was delighted!

Turtle had music, twinkling lights and an on/off button. Bear was just plain blue, and soft. He did not twinkle.

Bear was disappointed, again.

That next night after Max's Mom put Max to bed, while Turtle's music was playing and Turtle's lights were twinkling, Bear decided. He would wait! He would wait as long as it took for Max to love him.

Bear waited.

Max got **bigger**.

One night at dinner, Max tried a new food called an avocado. It was green, and smooth and very squishy! Max could smash it, Max could grab it, and Max could eat it all by himself! He ate a lot of avocado. Maybe Max ate too much avocado!

After dinner Max's Mommy gave Max a bath, read him stories and put Max to bed.

Then...

"WAAAAAAAAAAAAAAAAA AAAAAAAAAAAAAAAAAA AAAAAAAAAAAH!"

Max began to wail. He wailed and wailed and wailed. He had a bellyache.

Max's Mommy and Daddy raced into Max's room. They picked Max up. They rocked Max. They sang to Max. They tried Sophie's squeaking. They tried Turtle's music and twinkle lights. They tried everything to make Max feel better.

Max wailed.

Bear waited.

Max's Daddy spotted Bear. Max's Mommy spotted Bear. They stared at each other. Could it be? Could it be that Bear, who was plain blue and soft be the answer? Could he rescue Max?

Was Bear's waiting over?

Max's Mommy and Daddy picked Bear up and gave him to Max. Max hugged Bear, and because Bear was plain blue and soft, he could hug him, scrunch him and cuddle him without any squeaking, music, or twinkling. Max stopped wailing. Max was happy!

Max was happy. Max's Mom and Dad were happy. But, the happiest of all was Bear.

Bear had been
waiting for Max.

CPSIA information can be obtained
at www.ICGtesting.com
Printed in the USA
LVHW050937110223
739266LV00013B/863

9 781480 807907